Owlkids Books Inc.
10 Lower Spadina Avenue, Suite 400, Toronto, Ontario M5V 2Z2
www.owlkidsbooks.com

Distributed in Canada by University of Toronto Press
5201 Dufferin Street, Toronto, Ontario M3H 5T8

Distributed in the United States by Publishers Group West
1700 Fourth Street, Berkeley, California 94710

Library and Archives Canada Cataloguing in Publication

Whamond, Dave
    Oddrey / Dave Whamond.

Issued also in electronic format.
ISBN 978-1-926973-45-6

    I. Title.
PS8645.H34O33 2012   jC813'.6   C2011-907760-4

Library of Congress Control Number: 2011943509

Design: Barb Kelly

Canadian Heritage   Patrimoine canadien

Canada

Ontario
Ontario Media Development Corporation

Canada Council for the Arts   Conseil des Arts du Canada

ONTARIO ARTS COUNCIL
CONSEIL DES ARTS DE L'ONTARIO

Société de développement de l'industrie des médias de l'Ontario

We acknowledge the financial support of the Canada Council for the Arts, the Ontario Arts Council, the Government of Canada through the Canada Book Fund (CBF) and the Government of Ontario through the Ontario Media Development Corporation's Book Initiative for our publishing activities.

Manufactured by C&C Joint Printing Co., (Guangdong) Ltd.
Manufactured in Shenzhen, China, in April 2012
Job #HM1790

A   B   C   D   E   F

Owl kids   Publisher of Chirp, chickaDEE and OWL
www.owlkids.com

Oddrey

Written and illustrated by

DAVE WHAMOND

Owl
kids

Oddrey had always known
she wasn't like everybody else.

Her dad said she danced to the beat of her own drum.

Her mom said she always liked to do the unexpected.

Her dog, Ernie, said, "Meow."
(Even Oddrey's dog liked
to stand out from the crowd.)

Oddrey didn't mind being
different from the other kids.

She believed it was important
to think for herself.

But not everyone appreciated
her unique style.

Sometimes,
Oddrey felt lonely.

Still, she didn't let anything get her
down for long. Oddrey knew how
to make the best of any situation.

When her teacher told the class that they would be putting on a play, Oddrey was excited about starring in the show.

Okay, not "starring."
But "appearing"…

Despite her disappointment, Oddrey vowed to be the most unique tree ever.

But her teacher had other ideas.

On the night of the performance,
as Oddrey stood waiting for the curtain
to go up, she started to get a bad feeling.

DUH
DUH
DUH
DUH

Before long, Oddrey could see
that the play wasn't going well.

Milton forgot his lines. Amir was hiding behind a prop. And Trish…well, Trish was having a clumsy moment.

Oddrey knew that it was up to her to save the show.

And there wasn't a minute to lose.

"I don't remember any of that from rehearsal,"
said Oddrey's teacher.

"I improvised a bit," said Oddrey.

"You were supposed to be playing a tree,"
said her teacher.

Oddrey's teacher might not have appreciated her performance at first, but her classmates sure did.

After that night, Oddrey had to work
a bit harder to be different.

But somehow she managed.
Her name was **Oddrey** after all.